Julie Andrews Edwards
and Emma Walton Hamilton

LITTLE BO in ITALY

THE CONTINUED ADVENTURES OF BONNIE BOADICEA

ILLUSTRATED BY Henry Cole

An Imprint of HarperCollinsPublishers

Little Bo in Italy

Text copyright © 2010 by Wellspring LLC

Illustrations copyright © 2010 by Henry Cole

All rights reserved. Manufactured in China.

No part of this book may be used or reproduced in any manner whatsoever without written permission except in the case of brief quotations embodied in critical articles and reviews. For information address HarperCollins Children's Books, a division of HarperCollins Publishers, 10 East 53rd Street, New York, NY 10022.

www.harpercollinschildren.com

Library of Congress Cataloging-in-Publication Data

Edwards, Julie, date

Little Bo in Italy : The continued adventures of Bonnie Boadicea / Julie Andrews Edwards and Emma Walton Hamilton ; illustrated by Henry Cole. — 1st ed.

p. cm. — (Julie Andrews collection)

Summary: The little cat called Bonnie Boadicea and her owner find great adventure while traveling along the coast of Italy, where Bo continues to seek her siblings and find friendship wherever she goes.

ISBN 978-0-06-008908-5 (trade bdg.)

ISBN 978-0-06-008909-2 (lib. bdg.)

[1. Cats—Fiction. 2. Voyages and travels—Fiction. 3. Circus—Fiction. 4. Sisters—Fiction. 5. Italy—Fiction.] I. Cole, Henry, date, ill. II. Title.

PZ7.E2562Lii 2010   2009025442

[Fic]—dc22   CIP

AC

Typography by Rachel Zegar

10 11 12 13 14   SCP   10 9 8 7 6 5 4 3 2 1

❖

First Edition

For Captain Charlie, with love & thanks
—Julie & Emma

Per Penni, con felici ricordi di Roma e, naturalmente,
il monumento di Vittorio Emanuele!
—Hen

CONTENTS

CHAPTER ONE

A New Job

BILLY BATES LIFTED UP his little gray cat and gently rubbed her chin.

"Now, Bo," he said, and his voice sounded rather serious. "We are on a *real* yacht, and if you're going to be a proper ship's cat, then you'll have to really behave yourself from now on! This isn't a fishing boat like the *Red Betsy*. There is to be *no* sharpening of claws on anything—not the carpets, not the furnishings, not the decks. No attacking the curtains either. No playing with the lines." Then he added, "Those are the ropes, for your information."

Bo—short for Bonnie Boadicea—blinked innocently at Billy with her beautiful violet eyes. In the six months since the young sailor had rescued the abandoned kitten and made her his lucky mascot, they had been on many adventures together—and several boats. From the herring boat in England, where Billy was working when they met, to the ferry they took to France in search of a new job, to the comfy river barge upon which they hitched a ride south to the Mediterranean, she had always shown respect for her surroundings, and never once sharpened her claws on anything *important*.

(Except perhaps when she was cross . . . and even then it had only been on Billy's mattress or a sisal "Welcome" mat.)

Just two days ago, Billy had been signed on as extra crew aboard the beautiful motor sailer *Legend*. Lord Goodlad, the owner of the yacht, had hired Billy after he and Bo had foiled an attempt to kidnap Lord Goodlad's lovely wife, Jessie. It was the job Billy had always dreamed of, and Bo was very happy for him and felt that she could never live in a finer place. If only Mama and Papa could see her now! But Mama was back in England at the manor house where Bo was born, and who knows where Papa was, since he was such a wanderer. As to her brothers and sisters—well, Princess had stayed with Mama, but all the other kittens had scattered on the fateful night when they were nearly drowned by an evil butler.

Bo had no idea where they had all ended up, until, to her delight, she had run into her brother Tubs in Paris just a few weeks ago. He was living in comfort as a chef's cat—but Samson, Polly, and Maximillian were still somewhere out in the big world. She did so want to find out what had happened to them, and to know whether they had found happy homes and were as well taken care of as she was.

The motor sailer *Legend* was magnificent—every inch constructed for seaworthiness and comfort. Belowdecks to the rear, or "aft," of the boat, was the master cabin—the luxurious stateroom occupied by Lord and Lady Goodlad. Forward of that were two guest suites, one on each side of the yacht, and all three cabins were lavishly appointed.

Center of the lower deck was the engine room, where ship's engineer Wally Jones spent many hours. There wasn't a thing he didn't know about the working parts of the yacht—from her immaculate, white-painted engines to the electrical systems, fuel tanks, batteries, pumps, filters, and bilges to the water maker and even the washing machines in the laundry room next door.

Wally wore dirty, oil-covered overalls and a cap during the day, and his face was usually smeared with paint and whatever else he came into contact with. Only after he'd taken his evening shower was Bo able to see that he was of fair complexion, with short hair that stuck out from his head in untidy clumps and which he cut himself whenever he felt like it. He had a wicked sense of humor, and he and Billy hit it off right away. They shared a cabin in the crew's quarters, which were also belowdecks, forward in the narrow prow of the boat.

Marie-Claire, the enchantingly pretty young lady who worked full-time for the Goodlads, shared a second small cabin with Lucy, the ship's cheerful cook.

Above decks was the main lounge, or "saloon." Forward of that was the "galley," superbly fitted with every modern kitchen appliance, built-in cupboards, and a booth and table where the crew could take their meals. Just beyond was the dining room, with a spectacular view of the front of the yacht and the surrounding ocean.

A curved staircase led to a smaller deck above and the bridge—the command center where Captain Ian Fraser helmed the boat when she was under way. There was a large ship's wheel and every possible aid to safe sailing, plus chart tables and a comfortable raised sofa where the crew, or anyone, could sit when the lovely vessel was at sea.

Captain Ian was an elderly, white-haired Scotsman, tall, erect, thin.

Though quite proper in manner, he was kind and fair and had a droll wit. His private quarters were adjacent to the bridge. Beyond them, a small lounge opened onto the rear top deck.

Towering above all were the yacht's two magnificent masts, each carrying large booms that held trimly furled white sails.

Captain Ian summoned the crew to his quarters that morning.

"Right, everyone, we're going to be moving out a little sooner than expected. The Goodlads had a nasty shock a few days ago when Her Ladyship was almost kidnapped, and they are anxious to change location and have a relaxing spell at sea. In ten days, they will attend a gala at the British ambassador's villa in Rome. Meantime, we'll take a leisurely cruise down the Italian coast."

Bo pricked up her ears. She had heard Papa speak of Italy as one of the many places he had traveled. He had counseled his kittens not to be stay-at-home fireside cats, but rather to get out into the world and have adventures. Wouldn't he be pleased to know that she was doing just that! Besides, the more she traveled, the greater her chances were of finding out what had happened to her siblings.

"Wally, get your ducks in a row in the engine room," the captain was saying. "Lucy, stock up the usual goods—allowing for an extra crew mate, and something for a little cat, of course." The captain smiled, and continued, "Billy, check everything topside and let me know what you think. And give Lucy a hand with the shopping, will you? Marie-Claire—the usual chores . . . laundry, linens, flowers, and so forth. We'll depart Saturday at oh six hundred hours."

So began a busy few days. Billy scrubbed the decks and washed down the superstructure of the yacht and checked the sails, lines, and safety equipment. He accompanied Lucy to the market on several occasions, carrying her heavy shopping bags, and he helped Marie-Claire turn over the mattresses and air the linens.

He was polishing the brass saloon door handles one day, Bo at his side, when two men walked down the quay and paused in front of him.

"Hello! Ahoy there!" one of them called out.

"How is Lady Goodlad?" the other inquired. Billy recognized the two customers who had been in the restaurant on the night she was almost kidnapped.

"Her Ladyship is recovering, thank you," he said.

"Glad to hear that," declared the larger man of the two. "Are you heading out then?"

"Soon," Billy said, and moved to wipe the railing.

"Going far?" said the other man, who was tall, thin, and sallow faced.

"Oh, round and about." Billy rubbed at a spot vigorously.

"Just wondered if you'd be gone long," said the larger man. "We wanted to have a word with His Lordship."

"Oh? Is there a problem?" Billy looked at them more intently. "I don't believe I caught your names. . . . "

"No problem, just business. I'm Jack Haggard," replied the big man. "My partner here is Fred Pallid."

"What is the nature of your business?"

"We're in—marine research," said Haggard.

"Yeah. Big fish, mainly," said Pallid with a friendly grin. "We wanted to ask His Lordship's advice, seeing as he knows the area so well."

Captain Ian appeared on the top deck and called down. "Something amiss, Billy?"

Haggard waved a hand in dismissal. "Listen, this is probably not a good time. We were just inquiring after Lady Goodlad's health." He pointed at Bo. "That's a cute kitty-cat, by the way. Come on, Fred, we've got work to do."

When the men were out of earshot, Captain Ian said quietly, "Careful, Billy. You didn't tell them where we were heading, did you?"

"Not a word, sir."

"Good man."

Bo felt relief as the two strangers walked away. Something about them made her feel anxious, though she couldn't tell why. She began to wash herself, and she was just thinking of taking a relaxing nap when a familiar voice hailed her.

"*Bonjour, chérie!* Another day in paradise, *n'est-ce pas?*" It was Panache, the marmalade cat she had met on the river barge, who somehow kept showing up at the oddest times, mostly when she wasn't expecting to see him. She ran down the gangplank to the quay.

Billy glanced up from his work and smiled as he watched the two friends greet each other.

"So, what excitement has happened since last we met?" Panache flicked his tail with interest.

"You silly fellow, we saw each other just yesterday," Bo said.

"Yes, yes, I know . . . but you are a magnet for adventure, and I have an endless appetite for amusement!" He rolled onto his back, tapped her shoulder playfully, and added, "Tell me *everything!*"

"Actually, I do have a bit of news," Bo replied. "We're leaving soon."

Panache sat up. "*Vraiment?*" he said. "For where? And for how long?"

"I'm not sure how long we'll be gone—but we're going to Italy."

"Aah! Italia! Well. *Attention, chérie,* I hear the tomcats in that part of the world love to play Catsanova."

"Catsanova?"

"A cool cat, I'm told, who stole the heart of many a pretty kitty."

Bo lifted her chin. "I think I can take care of myself," she said with great

dignity. "But thank you for your concern. Anyway, I'm searching for news of my family. So meeting him, or any other cats for that matter, might be very helpful."

"And you leave when?"

"Tomorrow. Oh six hundred hours." Panache looked puzzled. "That's six o'clock in the morning, for your information."

The ginger cat shuddered. "Brrrr! Too early for me. So this must be good-bye."

"I suppose so. . . ." Bo hesitated.

Panache sniffed the air. "Well, it seems the weather will be good," he said. "*Bon voyage, ma petite.* Perhaps I will be here when you return. Perhaps not."

He jumped onto the harbor wall and sauntered away, his tail held high.

9

CHAPTER TWO

The Stowaway

CAPTAIN IAN PRESSED the starter buttons of the engines at exactly five forty-five the following morning. As they throbbed into life, the yacht shuddered momentarily, and in Billy's bunk, Bo awoke and wondered what was happening.

Billy and the rest of the crew had been up for an hour already, making sure everything was shipshape and safe for the journey ahead. They had stowed every movable object, locked the cupboards, gathered outdoor cushions and mats, and lashed down the folding deck chairs. Lucy provided fresh coffee and warm croissants for everyone. The gangplank was hauled aboard, lines were cast off, fenders were pulled in.

With great care, Captain Ian eased *Legend* out of her narrow slip and into the main thoroughfare of the harbor. As the beautiful yacht swung around, he thrust both engines into forward motion and slowly headed toward the mouth of the harbor and the Mediterranean Sea sparkling beyond.

A shout came from the breakwater. Monsieur Abelard, the florist, was standing there with his little donkey; also Cap'n Jed, who owned the Chinese junk *Black Fin* and Monsieur Le Gros, the harbormaster. On the bridge, Billy, with Bo in his arms, waved to them, and the men waved back. As *Legend* reached the open sea, her beautiful bow dipped into the waves. Bo twitched her nose as she inhaled the morning-fresh air, with its hint of salt spray, cedar and olive trees, rosemary, and just a whiff of engine fuel.

Billy said, "Good to be under way again, isn't it, Bo?" and she purred happily.

Lord Goodlad appeared on the bridge in his dressing gown.

"Couldn't ask for a better day!" he said, rubbing his hands. "Let's put up steadying sails, skipper. It'll give Her Ladyship a chance to sleep in and make a smoother ride during her breakfast."

Billy placed Bo in a sunny spot on the console, forward of the big ship's wheel. "Stay here, Bo, and watch what happens," he said. "You're in for a treat."

Captain Ian maneuvered *Legend* into the wind as Billy and Wally went forward to the prow and untied the bindings around the foresail. Within seconds, a huge sheet of white cloth appeared, flapping and fluttering until, caught by the breeze, it billowed and tightened into a gentle arc.

The boys moved aft to the mainsail, and unable to contain her curiosity, Bo jumped down and ran back through the small lounge to a spot where she could watch the second sail unfurl. As it began to climb the mast, something fell out from the folds of the material and landed with a soft thud on the deck.

"*Oof!*" said a familiar voice. It was Panache. He steadied himself, shuddered

in the breeze as it ruffled his fur, and shook his head in a puzzled fashion. "Hmm. Must have dropped off!" he said, blinking. "Where am I?"

Bo trotted forward. "Panache, you rascal!" she said. "Did you deliberately hide away?"

"Of course I didn't!" he said indignantly. "I found a safe place to sleep last night, and suddenly I'm rudely awakened and tipped out of my bed."

Billy noticed the ginger cat and picked him up. "What on earth are *you* doing here?" he said. "Are you chasing after my Bo?"

Wally exclaimed, "Whoops! That's a spanner in the works. I wonder if we'll have to turn back."

"Let's see what the skipper says," Billy replied.

On the bridge, Captain Ian said, "Oh, dear. I did wonder what baggage a ship's cat might bring—but I never expected this. I'll have to speak to the Goodlads."

Moments later, Billy, Captain Ian, and Lord and Lady Goodlad were gathered in the main saloon. Bo and Panache sat side by side on the rug, watching with interest as the new turn of events was discussed.

"Do you think he belongs to anyone?" Her Ladyship was asking.

"No, ma'am," Billy replied. "I'm afraid this fellow's been following us since Paris."

"*Really?*" She sounded surprised.

"So, our little Bo has a suitor!" Lord Goodlad joked. "What shall we do with the stowaway? Make him walk the plank?"

"Oh, Barney!" Lady Goodlad chided him. "We already have one cat on board. We certainly have room for another."

Lord Goodlad sighed. "Jessie! You and your penchant for cats!"

She looked at him coquettishly, and her lovely blue eyes sparkled with mischief. "But what choice do we have, darling? It's too late to turn back. Billy, take our new guest to the galley and give him a bite to eat. He's probably famished."

"I'm *terribly* sorry about this, sir," Billy apologized as he scooped both cats into his arms. "I do appreciate your kindness, and I'll take full responsibility for keeping them both out of your way."

"Rubbish! If I know my Jessie, they'll be sunning on the aft deck with her by lunchtime."

Bo watched as Panache hungrily attacked the plate of fish morsels that Lucy put down for him.

"You *knew* we were departing this morning," she said. "I told you last night. So why did you choose *our* sail to sleep in?"

"What? Oh, phooey! Let's not go on and on about this. Besides, aren't you pleased to see me?" He began to clean his whiskers.

Bo had to admit that she was.

* * *

As Lord Goodlad had predicted, the cats spent the rest of the day with Her Ladyship, enjoying the fresh sea air, the sun, and being spoiled.

The occasional luffing of the sails, the lazy rocking motion of the boat, the sough of the sea as it passed under *Legend's* keel were so relaxing that the cats couldn't help snoozing until Marie-Claire appeared with a late lunch of delicious sandwiches that Lucy had made for everyone.

The afternoon passed uneventfully. Silver fish leaped above the water line from time to time, and a few inquisitive seabirds wheeled overhead. Occasionally, a tanker, a fishing boat, or another yacht was spotted. Some of the vessels were large and magnificent, but Bo thought none were as pretty as *Legend*.

At dusk, a landmass appeared on the horizon.

Captain Ian told Lord Goodlad, "Livorno, dead ahead, sir. We'll be pulling into the harbor in just under an hour." He looked up as his words were almost drowned out by a loud sound overhead—the *whump, whump, clackety-clack* of a helicopter above that was flying in circles around them. The captain grabbed his binoculars, slid open the bridge door, and stepped outside for a closer look.

"Sir!" he called as the helicopter came into focus. "Someone is taking photographs of the yacht."

"That is *so* irritating!" Lord Goodlad followed to see for himself. "Probably the dratted press. Paparazzi, no doubt. How did they know where to find us? BACK OFF!" he yelled, waving his arms at the noisy intruder, and the helicopter peeled away and thundered into the distance.

CHAPTER THREE

A Trip to Pisa

THAT EVENING, with *Legend* safely moored in the old harbor and a picturesque medieval tower dominating the view, Captain Ian said to his crew, "The Goodlads will be staying here for at least two days, so as long as we take turns and two of us are aboard at all times, you can do a bit of sightseeing, if you wish. Billy, you've never seen Tuscany. I highly recommend a trip to Pisa. The Leaning Tower is a must-see, and it's a great drive up the coast. Why don't you take Marie-Claire with you tomorrow, once morning chores are done. Make a day of it."

Marie-Claire clapped her hands in delight. "*Quel amusement!* I will make a *pique-nique!*"

At bedtime, Billy stroked Bo's soft fur and said, "I'll be going ashore for a few hours tomorrow, little one. Now that your marmalade friend is with us, I think it's best if you both stay here—but promise me you'll keep out of trouble while I'm gone."

Bo didn't like the sound of that at all. Just because Panache had decided to come with them, that didn't mean she shouldn't continue to enjoy her adventures with Billy. Besides, how could she search for news of her family if she stayed on the boat all day?

To make matters worse, the following morning Panache was nowhere to be found. Bo wondered moodily what she was going to do with herself. The Goodlads had gone ashore, Lucy was cleaning the kitchen, and neither Wally nor Captain Ian seemed inclined to play.

Early that afternoon, Billy surprised Marie-Claire by pulling up to the yacht in a tiny rental car that had obviously seen better days. He tooted the horn, stepped out, and with a sweep of his hand said, "Your carriage awaits, milady!" Marie-Claire laughed as she ran down the gangplank, picnic basket in hand.

The journey was as lovely as Captain Ian had predicted. The little car rattled its way up the coast through picturesque villages with the sparkling ocean and dunes on one side and the Appian Alps in the distance. Arriving

at the mouth of the historic Arno River, Billy swung the car right and followed the river all the way to Pisa.

The famed Leaning Tower was easy to find, and Billy and Marie-Claire were enthralled as they pulled up to a grassy expanse where the fabled circular bell tower stood, gleaming in the sunlight. Eight stories high and made of white marble, the Leaning Tower resembled a tiered wedding cake, with arches and pillars on each level. The whole edifice was definitely tilted at a rather alarming angle.

"Just amazing!" said Billy. "They say you can climb to the top. Shall we?"

"I hope it doesn't fall over!" Marie-Claire laughed. "Let us have our *pique-nique* first. I think we will need our strength."

Billy found a parking space, and they took the picnic basket from the trunk, locked the car, and strolled across the piazza. There were a number of tourists, but they found a suitable spot and spread their blanket on the grass.

"This is called the Square of Miracles," Billy said, reading from his guidebook as Marie-Claire opened the hamper. "The tower is almost a thousand years old and took a hundred and seventy-seven years to build. . . ." He looked up as Marie-Claire gave a startled gasp.

"*Mon Dieu!* What is this? Look, Billee!"

Nestled between the sandwiches and the flask of coffee, feeling very pleased with herself, was Bo. She jumped out of the basket, stretched, then rubbed her head on Billy's knee.

"You *minx!*" he said. "What am I going to do with you? I guess you'll be in my jacket pocket for the rest of the day."

The delicious picnic was consumed and a few morsels shared with Bo. Billy brushed the crumbs from his lap. "Right! Up we go!"

Two hundred ninety-something winding and well-worn steps later, they arrived at the parapet of the Leaning Tower, breathless but triumphant. They gazed at the colorful vista of terra-cotta rooftops, the river, and the Alps beyond.

22

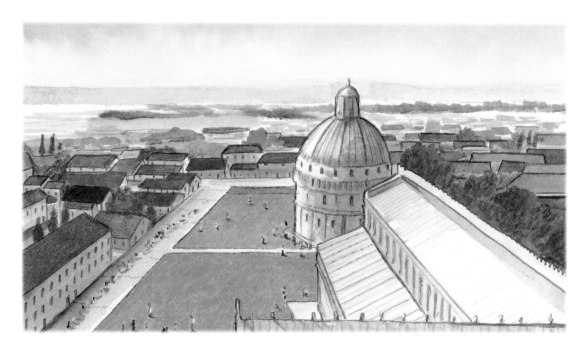

"*Regardez!* You can see the sea, and the harbor at Livorno!" Marie-Claire pointed out. Bo wondered what Panache was doing at that moment.

Turning around, they peered down at the seven large bells on the floor below.

"Apparently each one corresponds to a note in the musical scale," Billy read from his book, "and it takes fourteen people to make them all ring! Don't worry, Bo," he said, chuckling, "they're only rung on special occasions and holidays."

Back in the piazza, they decided to explore the nearby streets and shops. Canopied stalls displayed souvenirs, trinkets, postcards, and colorful paintings and posters announcing all manner of events.

One advertisement in particular seemed to be pasted everywhere. Its bold lettering read:

CIRCO SPLENDIDO Presente . . . GREGORIO e i suoi Grandi Gatti!

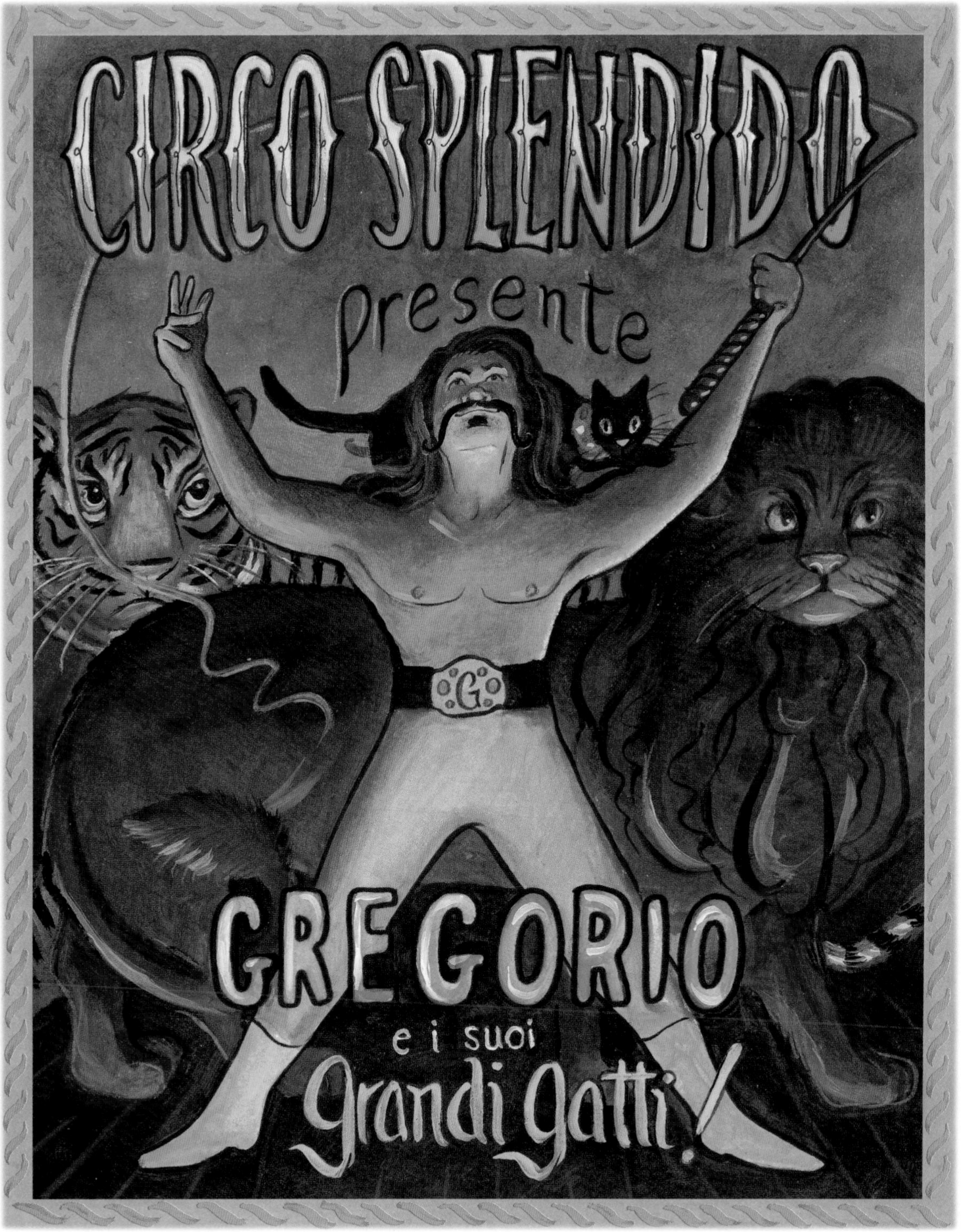
CIRCO SPLENDIDO
presente
GREGORIO
e i suoi
Grandi Gatti!

There was a dramatic picture of a muscular gentleman with a magnificent handlebar mustache. Bare chested and wielding a whip, he was surrounded by a ferocious-looking lion and a large striped tiger. But Bo's attention was riveted to the magnificent black cat that was perched on his shoulders. She studied the image. The cat wore a jewel-encrusted gold collar. Tilting her head to one side, she thought, "How like Papa he looks!"

"Oh, Billy!" Marie-Claire exclaimed. "A *cirque!* Can we go?"

"I do like the circus . . . ," Billy replied. He studied the address. "It's not far from Livorno. Let's see if we can find it on our way back." Bo's heart skipped a beat. Perhaps she could meet that black cat and find out more about him.

An hour later they were strolling the campgrounds where the traveling circus had set up its main tent, caravans, and trucks. Munching on peanuts, Billy and Marie-Claire admired the gently swaying elephants tethered to their stakes and allowed them to grasp a nut or two with their inquisitive trunks. There were ponies wearing brightly colored plumes and clowns selling programs and refreshments. Peeking out from Billy's jacket, Bo scanned her surroundings, but there was no sign of the black cat from the poster.

They approached several cages. One held a tiger, and in another several lionesses were pacing restlessly back and forth. A large lion with an impressive mane was lounging in a smaller enclosure. He gave a mighty yawn, displaying an awesome mouthful of sharp teeth. Bo dug her claws into Billy's jacket.

"Steady, Bo." Billy caught her as she scrambled toward his shoulder in panic. "You're safe with me."

A passing clown wearing an orange wig with a big red smile painted on his face wagged a finger at them.

"*Attento, signore!*" he warned. "The big one has the toothache. . . . Nimrod is *not* a happy *leone*."

Billy crossed to a ticket kiosk and purchased two seats for the evening's performance.

Bo felt a familiar prickle on the back of her neck, a sure sign that something was wrong. Looking around, she saw at once what it was. Lurking behind a nearby popcorn cart were the men she had last seen on the quay in France—Jack Haggard and Fred Pallid. They were whispering to each other and pointing at Marie-Claire and Billy.

A loudspeaker crackled, and a blaring voice announced, "*Signore e signori*, ladies and gentlemen! Please take your seats . . . *prendete i vostri posti!* The show is about to begin!"

Bo wondered how she could convey to Billy that she had seen the two men, but he was already striding toward the big top, Marie-Claire at his side—and the men were now nowhere in sight.

CHAPTER FOUR

The Circus

BILLY AND MARIE-CLAIRE climbed the steps of a large wooden riser and took their bench seats.

Bo, in Billy's lap, gazed at a big ring filled with sawdust. Colorful bright lights were strung above it, and a pair of closed red curtains hung at the back. A small orchestra seated in a balcony above played lustily.

All of a sudden, with a fanfare of trumpets, the curtains parted and several clowns spilled into the circle with whistles, ratchets, and kazoos. They threw handfuls of confetti at the crowd. Two of them carried buckets of water and pretended to douse the audience, but ended up dousing each other instead. Another juggled rubber clubs, and yet another threw large silver rings into the air and deftly caught them. One rode a unicycle around the rim of the ring, tooting a horn and teetering wildly toward the onlookers.

The orchestra blasted away, and now acrobats and tumblers appeared, dressed in white with sparkling sequined waistcoats. A young ballerina in a pink tutu danced out to pirouette in the center of the ring. She was followed by a tall man in black trousers, high boots, a bright red tailcoat, and a top hat. He sported a large, curling mustache and carried a long whip. Billy and Marie-Claire recognized him as the man they had seen on the poster in town. He seemed to be in charge, for he spread his arms wide as if to welcome everyone. Then, turning his back to the audience, he beckoned.

Through the velvet curtains lumbered the huge elephants with colorful beaded triangles on their heads, each one holding another's tail as they padded around the ring. They were followed by six white ponies, their harnesses decked with shiny gold tassels. As the elephants spun in individual circles, the prancing ponies wove wider circles around them. A troupe of performing dogs, barking and leaping happily, came next—guided by a lady, who made them walk on their hind legs and then jump up on the backs of the ponies.

One elephant lifted the little ballerina with his trunk and placed her high on his shoulders, just behind his big, flapping ears. She stood, balancing first on one leg, then the other, all the while waving at the crowd, who were clapping and cheering enthusiastically.

The ringmaster cracked his whip, making Bo jump nervously. In unison, the elephants and ponies rose up on their haunches and pawed the air. Billy and Marie-Claire were clapping so hard that Bo moved to sit on the bench between them. She craned her neck, hoping for a glimpse of the big black cat—but he was still nowhere in sight.

As the animals departed the ring, ropes and wires spun down from the ceiling and the acrobats began their long climb to the trapezes swaying above. Bo titled her head back so far that she nearly fell over, watching as they swung between the bars, catching one another in midair and somersaulting from one pair of hands to another. One of them walked across a taut, narrow wire that stretched the width of the tent, holding a colorful umbrella for balance and even performing a forward roll, then a backward one.

Meanwhile, tumblers were setting up the ring below with a trampoline and teeter-totters. They began their act by standing on one another's shoulders and making a pyramid of their bodies. One jumped on the end of a teeter-totter to send another sailing into the air, only to land on yet another's shoulders. They spun and whirled, calling out to each other with "HUPs!" and "HI-YAHs!" and ending with dramatic flourishes that encouraged the audience to applaud even louder.

The little dogs returned, dressed in fancy costumes. They jumped through hoops and ran up and down ladders. They balanced cups on their noses and walked on their hind legs along a narrow beam. They jumped and danced in time to the music of the orchestra and played tag around their trainer. One pretended to be so sleepy that he could not be roused until it was time for his bow, when he acted quite giddy with delight.

The elephants came out again, performing seemingly impossible tasks—like balancing on small drums, then sitting on them like stools, and placing their front feet on one another's haunches to form a line.

The ponies returned also, weaving around one another with precision timing in synchronized patterns. They bowed, one front leg extended, the other tucked beneath them, their heads dipped. The little ballerina balanced on their backs as they galloped and spun, and she was joined by the tumblers, who formed new pyramids, this time on top of the jogging ponies.

Billy joked with Marie-Claire, "I shall expect a good deal more from Bo after this!"

There was a crash of cymbals and a roll of drums, and the lights dimmed to a single spotlight. The clowns quickly brought in large sheets of steel fencing and began to assemble them to form a circle around the ring. The loudspeaker announced, "Ladies and gentlemen, *signore e signori!* We present Gregorio Bonoface and his *Grandi Gatti.* . . . First, his special friend, Pantera!"

Into the spotlight came the mustachioed ringmaster, now bare chested to reveal his rippling muscles. He wore gold spandex trousers, gold boots, and an oversized, bejeweled belt around his waist. On his shoulder was the spectacular black cat, so large that he resembled a small panther. Bo suddenly sat up very tall. The cat was indeed the very image of Papa, though considerably bigger. The ringmaster lifted Pantera with one arm, extending him way above his head, and then he spun the animal around as if he were twirling a baton. He threw him high, then caught him and

placed him on the ground. The man beat his chest, and light as a feather, the cat sprang in a single leap to his shoulder again.

Bo felt the hair on her back stand on end as something slowly dawned on her.

Presenting Pantera to the audience and signaling for them to pay close

attention, Gregorio took several deep, hissing breaths, then hurled the cat like a javelin through the air—and, miraculously, he landed on the high wire and stayed there, way above the crowd, his tail fluffed and upright for balance.

Billy leaped to his feet, applauding wildly, and Bo fell straight through the gap between the wooden bench and its riser. As she hit the dusty ground below with a thud, she suddenly knew why the cat Pantera resembled her father—he was in fact her long-lost beloved brother Samson.

Torn between finding her way back to Billy and rushing to greet Samson, Bo meowed loudly—but the stamping feet of the enthusiastic crowd above her, plus the noise of the orchestra, drowned out her cries. Scrambling to get out from under the seats, she made a dash for the sawdust aisle. She emerged into the bright lights and was momentarily dazzled. Pausing, she heard a voice say, "Hey! There's that kitty-cat from the sailboat again!"

Looking up, Bo discovered that Jack Haggard was right next to her. His rough hands reached out to pick her up, but with a hiss she wriggled away and ran to her right, then upon seeing the audience changed her mind and doubled back.

"Get her!" said the man called Fred. "She might be useful!"

Both men dropped to their knees, attempting to block her way, but Bo leaped over them and ran straight into the big arena just as the clowns rattled the last piece of steel fencing into place with a loud *clang!*

There was a deafening roar, and, frozen with fear, Bo found herself gazing into the cavernous jaws of the mighty lion Nimrod.

35

CHAPTER FIVE

A Memorable Performance

Bo's common sense finally returned. She backed away, hoping to slip between the rods of the steel fence. To her dismay, she found they were encased in mesh netting on the outside. Frantic, she decided to climb straight up instead. She got halfway, only to discover that she was unable to hook her claws into the shiny steel bars, and very slowly, she began to slide downward.

"HEL-L-L-P!" she meowed as loudly as she could. Looking wildly about her, she saw that the three lionesses and the striped tiger were also in the ring, and all of them, including Gregorio and Samson—or Pantera—were gazing up at her in astonishment.

From his seat in the risers, Billy gasped. "My Lord—that's *Bo!*" He looked at the bench beside him, then back at the ring. "She was just— how did she . . . ?" Grasping Marie-Claire's hand, he pushed and stumbled past other audience members to get to the aisle, tripping over their feet and knees in his haste. "'Scuse me! Pardon me! *So* sorry!" he stammered as he went. "That's *my* little cat out there!" No one seemed to understand what he was saying.

In the ring, Samson was calling in amazement, "Bo? Is that you? Is that *really* you?" There was a loud crack of the whip, and Bo lost her hold entirely—falling to the ground just as the lionesses and tiger leaped to take their places on wooden stools that had been placed around the ring.

Nimrod had circled the perimeter, and now he loped toward Bo. The huge cat kept shaking his head, trying to rid himself of the pain caused by his bad tooth.

Gregorio shouted, "Hey-a, Pantera!" and Samson leaped onto the lion's back, riding him as nimbly as the little ballerina had ridden the ponies.

Bo scrambled back in an attempt to get out of his way, but Samson called out, "Bo! Get up here! *Quick!* Jump up beside me!" Her eyes widened in horror. "*Bo!* For the love of Bast, do as I say! You're safer up here than down there!"

Nimrod gave a deafening roar, and at the sight of his glistening teeth, Bo took a leap of faith and sprang upward to join her brother on the lion's back. Samson flanked her with his paws as the large beast shook his mane, angry at having to carry an extra passenger.

"Whatever happens, *hang on!*" Samson yelled into her ear.

Bo shut her eyes and dug her claws into Nimrod's fur, clinging for all she was worth. She was vaguely aware of the music playing, the whip cracking, and the crowd cheering wildly at this unusual spectacle . . . but she didn't hear Billy, who was by now spread-eagled against the bars of the cage, desperately trying to get the lion tamer's attention.

"*Signore!* That's my cat!" He was shouting and pointing. "*Mia gatta!*"

Gregorio looked quickly in his direction, then back at his lions, who, curious about Bo, were becoming restless and pawing the air. He shrugged his shoulders at Billy as if to say, "What can I do?" Turning back to his troupe, he yelled, "Delilah! Vesta! Sheba! Tatiana!" He pointed to the ground, and the lionesses and tiger jumped down and lined up in front of him.

"R-R-R-R-R-R-ROLITO!" he commanded, and as one, they lay on the ground and rolled over on their backs. "Nimrod! *Per favore!*" He pointed his whip again, and the great lion, with the two cats on his back, took a flying leap across them all.

"*Ancora!* And again!"

The lionesses and tiger rolled in the opposite direction. Nimrod reversed course and, roaring his disapproval, leaped over them a second time.

Bo slipped precariously to one side and screamed, "SAM-SON!" Her brother grabbed her by the scruff of the neck and hauled her back into position.

"You *must* stay with me, Bo!" he yelled.

"Make him stop *roaring!*" she pleaded, her bones rattling as she was

39

bounced and jostled around.

"He's got a *toothache!*" Samson shouted. "He's really a trouper!"

Bo hissed, for now two of the lionesses had risen up on their haunches and placed their paws together to form an arch over Nimrod's back. The pink pads on their toes were as big as Bo's head, and she could feel their hot breath on her whiskers.

With another crack of the whip, the lionesses dispersed, and Nimrod began loping around the ring once more. Gregorio produced a large silver hoop and held it out in front of him. "*Salto!*" he shouted. "JUMP!"

Nimrod obeyed, and whimpering, Bo struggled to maintain her balance as the three cats soared through the air.

"*E ancora!*" cried the lion tamer, this time offering a larger hoop covered in white paper. There was a resounding *crack!* as Nimrod burst through the parchment, and Bo momentarily saw stars.

The lionesses snarled and swiped at Nimrod as he passed, and his tail swished back and forth with annoyance. Gregorio scooped the wooden stools together to form a set of steps and presented the largest ring of all, placing it squarely between them. He struck a giant match, and Billy, shaking the fencing, cried out "NO-O-O!" as he guessed what was about to come next.

"EHH! The *grande finale!*" the ringmaster yelled, touching the match to the giant hoop, which exploded into flames.

The orchestra stopped playing. The drums rolled. Bo began wailing at the top of her lungs.

"It's the big finish, Bo!" Samson shouted. "You can do it! Do it for Papa!"

She summoned her last reserves of courage and held fast as Nimrod ascended the steps and took to the air. The heat blasted like a furnace, and the angry flames licked at the cats, singeing Bo's whiskers as they passed through the inferno. The crowd thundered with applause as Nimrod landed surefootedly on the other side.

"Told you he was a trouper!" Samson grinned, and Bo felt a rush of relief at having survived the ordeal, and then just the tiniest thrill at being a part of the magic known as show business.

CHAPTER SIX

The Lion Tamer

THE LIONS AND TIGER were hustled out of the ring, and as Nimrod passed Gregorio, the ringmaster scooped Samson up in one arm and Bo in the other. He held them both aloft, acknowledging the crowd, who gave him a standing ovation.

Time and again he bowed, and as the steel fencing surrounding him was dismantled, Billy and Marie-Claire rushed forward. Billy grabbed Bo and held her to him. She burrowed her head into his neck.

"Oh, my Bonnie! Are you all right, little one?" he crooned, examining her from head to tail. He was quite oblivious to the fact that the entire company had entered the ring for the final bows, and they were now surrounded by ponies, elephants, dogs, clowns, and acrobats.

Gregorio placed an arm around Billy's shoulders and grabbed his hand, thrusting it upward and making him wave to the audience. The spotlight was blinding, people were thumping Billy on the back, and the dogs were leaping up to get a closer look at Bo. The orchestra played boisterously as Billy, Bo, and Marie-Claire found themselves in a procession of circus performers and animals, who marched once around the circle and then headed

43

toward the exit. The dense throng, and the occasional nudge from an elephant's trunk, gave them no choice but to be swept along, between the red curtains to the backstage area, where handlers were lined up to receive the animals.

There was a babble of Italian voices, and everybody seemed to be asking questions at once.

"I am *so* sorry!" Billy apologized breathlessly to Gregorio. "I don't know *how* she got into the ring. . . . One moment she was beside me, the next she was gone!"

Gregorio, still carrying Samson, interrupted him. "*Non si scusi!*" he bellowed, thumping him on the back. "Was the *best* performance we ever had! Come! We celebrate!" He ushered them into a nearby caravan. "Is *modesto*, but is home!"

The old trailer was made of wood and had a bowed roof. It was painted red with gold trim inside and out. There were faded satin curtains at the windows, a built-in convertible sofa, and a table with booth seating. An oil lamp hung from the ceiling, and a small gas stove nearby was covered in dirty pots and pans. The walls were pasted with yellowed photographs of Gregorio in various poses with lions and celebrities. There was a pungent smell of sweat, garlic, tomato sauce, and alcohol.

Gregorio rummaged in a cooler. "First, the *bambini!*" he said. He produced a carton of milk and poured the creamy liquid into a large saucer for Samson and Bo. He then pulled a half-full bottle of clear liquid from an overhead cupboard. Splashing the contents into three tumblers, he handed one each to Billy and Marie-Claire and raised his own in a toast.

"A *fortuna!*" he said, and downed the drink in one gulp.

Billy and Marie-Claire glanced at each other, sipped the liquid gingerly, and immediately felt a fire in their bellies.

"Sit! Sit!" Gregorio pointed to the booth. "Now, we talk! How much you want?"

"Excuse me?" Billy asked.

"How much? *Quanto?* For the leetle cat?"

"Oh—but she's not for sale . . . ," Billy stammered.

"*Bah!* Everything has a price! I *must* have her! I am mad for her!"

"I'm terribly sorry, sir—Bo belongs to me. I would never sell her."

Gregorio clutched his heart in mock despair. "*Sono desolato!* She is a tiny *gatta* with *grande coraggio.* Circo Splendido would have a new star. We make much money!"

Billy smiled. "I rather think that after the excitement of tonight, the Circo Splendido will find itself doing very well," he said.

"Yes!" Marie-Claire nodded. "Word will travel—or it will be in the newspapers!"

Bo and Samson lapped the last drop of milk from the saucer, then sat back and gazed at each other with delight.

"As I live and breathe, Bo! You gave me such a shock!" Samson wiped his face with his paw. "How in the world did you get to Italy?"

"I came on a boat! How did *you* get here?" Bo countered.

"Long story," Samson replied. "Short version is . . . remember when all us kittens were nearly drowned in the river? Polly and I escaped together.

We finally settled at the train station. . . . It gave us shelter and the occasional scrap of food dropped by travelers. Gregorio here was on holiday in England, and he spotted us under a bench on the platform. Being the cat lover that he is, he took pity on us and brought us back to Italy—"

"*Polly's* here?" Bo interrupted him excitedly.

"Well, yes and no," Samson replied. "She was never crazy about the circus—she was fragile, as you know, and the lions frightened her as much as they did you. She fell in love with a mangy Mau in Florence . . . a wolf in cat's clothing if ever I saw one. The next thing I knew, she'd run off with him. I haven't seen her since." The big black cat sighed. "But what about you?" He brightened. "Tell me *your* story."

Bo told him how she had met Billy, become a ship's cat, and traveled with him to France. "And you'll never guess, Samson! I met Tubs in Paris! He's a chef's cat now, and he's *so* happy!"

Samson grinned. "Oh! He *would* be. He always loved to eat! Any news of Maximillian?"

She shook her head. "None. But I'm determined to find out, even if it takes a lifetime of travels to do it!"

"But how did you come to be here tonight?" Samson asked.

"Billy and I, and that pretty lady, Marie-Claire, took a day off to do some sightseeing and saw your poster," Bo explained. "Billy works for a very important gentleman, who owns the boat we live on. His wife loves cats—she even took in a friend of mine from the South of France. His name is Panache."

Samson raised his eyebrows. "Not a mangy Mau, I hope?"

"Certainly not!" said Bo indignantly. "He's a very civilized marmalade. Besides, we're part of the ship's crew. We'll be sailing to Rome in a day or so."

"Well, isn't that the cat's meow! We're going to Rome too! We'll be performing there next week."

"Gosh, Samson . . . I don't know how you do what you do!"

"Eight shows a week." Samson flexed his muscles. "Twice a day on the weekends! It's a good life, once you put your back into it. Keeps me in shape."

"But what about those lions?" Bo shuddered. "Nimrod could have swallowed me whole!"

"Aw, he's a softy, really. Being fierce is all part of the act. Anyway, they're all just cats, like you and me—'cept they're bigger, of course."

"Well, I hope he gets over his toothache soon," Bo said uneasily.

"You were very brave tonight," Samson said with affection. "Mama and Papa would be proud."

"I thought *you* were Papa when I saw you on the poster. You are *so* like him." Bo sighed. "I hate to say good-bye. But at least I know where you are now, and that you're safe."

"We'll meet again one day, I'm sure," Samson said. Both cats sat in silence for a moment, lost in thought.

Billy stood up. "We really must head back to the yacht, sir. The skipper will be looking for us. Thank you for your kindness."

Gregorio took his hand and pumped it vigorously.

"*Arrivederci, amico!*" He picked up Bo and planted a smacking kiss on the top of her head. "*Ciao, bella!*" Handing her over to Billy, he added, "If you change your mind, my offer is standing on the table."

Driving back, Billy and Marie-Claire chatted nonstop about the events of the day and the extraordinary turn the evening had taken. Upon reaching the harbor, Billy dropped Marie-Claire and Bo at *Legend's* gangplank and headed off to return the car. Bo immediately went looking for Panache and found him sulking on the aft deck.

"Where have you *been?*" he said moodily. "I've been looking for you all day! Off on one of your adventures, no doubt. . . ."

"Wait till you hear, Panache!" Bo could hardly contain her excitement. "I've been to the top of a *huge* tower that was nearly falling over. Then we went to the circus, where I went into the lion's cage and found my brother Samson! I rode on the biggest lion's back, and we jumped over more lions and a tiger and through a fiery hoop!"

He looked at her a moment. "No, *vraiment*. What *have* you been doing?"

"It's the truth!" Bo laughed. "How was *your* day?"

50

"Oh, *très amusant*," he said drily. "I went to the fish market and poked about. I came back and took a catnap. I watched the ferry docking. . . ."

Bo curled up beside him. "Poor Panache! I did look for you this morning."

"*Zut alors!*" Panache said gloomily. "I miss all the fun. I will have to stay closer from now on."

Bo yawned. The day had certainly been adventurous, but it felt good to be safely back on the yacht. Images of the circus flashed through her mind . . . the ponies, the elephants, Gregorio and the lions. How wonderful it had been to find Samson there! And how brave and strong he had grown to be! Had it not been for him, she would never have found the courage to face up to the lions as she had. She suddenly felt rather pleased with herself. Not even Papa, in all his travels, had ever spoken about meeting a lion face-to-face. She wished she could tell him.

And what of Polly, her shy and sensitive sister? . . . Where could she be now? To know that she was *somewhere* in Italy—so near, perhaps—yet not to be able to see her was frustrating. Bo hoped she was all right, and made a promise to herself that she would never stop searching for her remaining brother and sister.

Suddenly, Bo remembered seeing Haggard and Pallid at the circus. What was it about them that made her feel so uneasy? They had certainly behaved mysteriously. If only she could have told Billy.

CHAPTER SEVEN

The Islands

TWO DAYS LATER, *LEGEND* pulled out of the harbor at Livorno and sailed a leisurely afternoon cruise to the lovely island of Elba. Lord Goodlad took the helm for the pleasure of it, and since the journey was short, they opted to cross under sail as opposed to using the engines. *Legend* heeled over to a gentle twenty-degree angle and cut through the waters with silent grace.

Billy and Wally were kept busy trimming the sails as needed to accommodate the wind. Everyone was relaxed and happy, and there was much talk of Bo's adventures at the circus. Lady Goodlad seemed to be over her recent scare, and no mention was made of the plot to kidnap her. She seemed particularly delighted to have Bo and Panache aboard, for they proved to be wonderful companions for her, and their playful antics kept her amused.

A few hours later, *Legend* eased into a slip at Portoferraio, Elba. Everything seemed color filled and so different from anything Bo had seen back in England. The buildings were pink or mustard colored, and all were topped by terra-cotta roof tiles. Some of the doors were bright blue, and the windows had green shutters that were tipped upward. A lighthouse stood on the promontory, and next to it was an old, rose-colored fort, which glowed in the sunset. On the hillsides, ancient walls built thousands of years ago conveyed a sense of history, safety, and strength.

Several boats were anchored in the harbor. A ferry from the mainland was coming in, and a large cruise ship was moored nearby. "Too many tourists tonight," Captain Ian remarked to Lucy. "So we'll eat aboard—but tomorrow the Goodlads will take us all out to dinner. There's a grand little restaurant on the quay."

Supper that night was served on the aft deck. Bo and Panache lounged on the banquette, listening drowsily to the conversation of the Goodlads as they ate and discussed the great emperor Napoleon, who had once been exiled on the island.

"Amazing to think he spent nine months here, with a gorgeous mansion, a force of six hundred troops, and a lady to keep him company, and all he could think about was getting back to France!" said Lady Goodlad.

Her husband smiled at her. "Some people just don't appreciate what they've got," he said. "I'd spend the rest of my life here with *you*." She touched his hand tenderly.

The following morning the cruise ship departed, and the harbor was peaceful and inviting. Marie-Claire and Billy explored the narrow streets and alleyways behind the marina, visited Napoleon's historic home, and did some shopping, purchasing local wine that Lord Goodlad had requested.

Later, the entire crew joined the Goodlads at a restaurant on the quay. They secured a table outside with a breathtaking view. A group of local lads passed by, their arms linked in friendship. The delicious dinner included fresh-made pizzas, pasta, and fresh grilled sardines—some of which Billy took back to the boat as a treat for Bo and Panache.

Legend put out to sea the next day and sailed on down the Italian coast. Several hours later, the profile of a majestic mountain came into view. Glancing at the map on the chart table, Billy saw that what he thought was an island was actually a peninsula.

"It's called Monte Argentario," Captain Ian explained, "which translates roughly to 'silver mountain'—probably because of how it looks at sunset." He steered *Legend* into an unspoiled natural cove, where they dropped anchor for the night. The translucent water alternated from turquoise to emerald, from aquamarine to cobalt blue. The land around them was dotted with Mediterranean scrub and rock roses, and the air was richly fragrant with the perfume of thyme, myrtle, wild olive, and fig.

Billy picked up Bo and stroked her head. "Look, Bo . . . have you ever seen water so crystal clear or so beautiful?" he marveled.

"Feel like a swim, Billy?" Captain Ian inquired.

"*May* I, sir?"

Billy rushed to his cabin to change into his trunks and moments later was splashing in the warm sea. With shouts of merriment, Wally and Marie-Claire joined him. Bo looked cautiously from the top of the steps to see what all the fun was about.

"Come on, Bo!" Billy encouraged. "Come down!" Bo hesitated. "That's my girl! You can do it!"

Very tentatively, Bo moved to the next step, then the next. Reaching the bottom of the ladder, she tapped the water gingerly with one paw. Shaking it, she licked at her wet fur and discovered that its salty taste was quite pleasant. Billy urged her on, and she braced herself, then took a giant leap— right into his arms.

"Clever girl!" he said, and eased her into the water. "Now you're a *real* ship's cat!"

Wally and Marie-Claire clapped delightedly as Bo suddenly found her

sea legs and struck out. To her surprise, swimming felt wonderful. She swam a few circles around Billy, then made her way back to the boat. Shaking the water from her fur, she looked up to see Panache peeping at her over the lip of the swim ladder.

"Your turn, Panache!" she said cheekily.

Panache shuddered. His ears pressed to his head, he said emphatically, "*Non, merci!*" and disappeared from view.

Lady Goodlad came down the steps with a warm towel for Bo. There was a thunderous splash as Lord Goodlad swan dived from the deck of the boat into the water.

He surfaced, spluttering a bit. Brushing drops of water from her blouse, his wife called to him, "Beautiful, darling! You've still got it!"

Between the day's sailing, the fresh air, the swimming, and Lucy's sumptuous supper, sleep came easily to all on board that night, and *Legend* rocked gently under the stars.

CHAPTER EIGHT

Rome

BILLY WAS BESIDE HIMSELF with excitement as *Legend* and her crew docked in Fiumicino, the port of Rome.

"Just imagine, Bo!" he said as he tied off the last line securing *Legend* to the quay. "We're actually in *Rome* . . . one of the founding cities of Western civilization! It's only been a few months since we left that smelly old herring boat—who could have guessed that our fortunes would lead us *here*?"

Captain Ian leaned over the railing. "Billy!" he called. "The British embassy has provided us with one of their cars for the length of our stay. Her Ladyship needs to go into the city to get her hair and nails done for the gala this evening. Obviously, her safety is essential—she'd prefer that *you* drive, and Marie-Claire accompany her. With the diplomatic plates, you shouldn't have a problem parking anywhere. Be ready in half an hour?"

"Aye aye, skipper!"

"*Bonjour*, Billy!" Marie-Claire called to him, her pretty face framed in the galley window. "Isn't it exciting? We will see Rome! My favorite city!"

"How many times have you been here?"

"Twice. For me, it is the most romantic place in the world."

"Not Paris?" he teased.

"Well, it's—how you say—Steven even!"

Billy chuckled. "You mean it's a tie?"

"That also." She wrinkled her nose at him and shut the window.

Billy programmed Lady Goodlad's destination into the car's navigation system. Her Ladyship came down the gangplank, followed by Marie-Claire and Captain Ian.

"This is good of you both," Lady Goodlad said. "Barney has absolutely no interest in hanging about while I'm under the hair dryer; however, *you* two might like to potter about the city during that time. Marie-Claire, I was hoping you could pick up some shoes for me—they're being held at a shop near the salon."

As Billy opened the car door for the ladies, Bo jumped in ahead of everyone. Billy shook his head.

"No, no, little one. You need to stay on the boat today. . . . Back you go!"

Bo was appalled. Did Billy intend to leave her behind from now on? What of her quest to find news of her family?

"Give her to me," Captain Ian suggested.

Bo dug her claws into the fabric of the car's seat, determined not to budge.

"Oh, let her come, Billy," Lady Goodlad entreated. "She'll be safer with us than on board. If doors are left open, Bo will probably go looking for you, and I wouldn't want her locked up in a cabin all day."

"Are you sure, milady?"

"*Quite* sure." She picked Bo up and set her on her lap. Bo blinked her big violet-colored eyes at Billy and purred.

Suddenly, Panache leaped into the car and planted himself firmly on the seat beside them. Leaning against Lady Goodlad, he looked up at her adoringly.

"Yes, yes, you rascal. You can come too!" she said, laughing.

Captain Ian glanced at Billy and raised his eyes heavenward.

"*Panache!*" Bo whispered. "What do you think you're *doing?*"

"I told you, *chérie*, I am not going to miss any more adventures!"

"I don't think there'll *be* any adventures," Bo said. "I just want to be with my Billy."

"Mm-hmm," he said contentedly. "We'll see!"

Billy started the car.

"Take it easy, Billy," Captain Ian said. "Driving in Rome takes a certain skill. Everyone on the streets has his own agenda—so keep your wits about you." He thumped his hand on the roof. "Off you go."

Billy took the captain's advice, which was just as well—for traffic seemed to come from all directions. Cars overtook them at alarming speeds, often in the wrong lane. Scooters and mopeds buzzed around and in front of them, ignoring red lights and going in the wrong direction down one-way streets. Pedestrians stepped out in front of the car with no thought for their own safety. Fortunately, Billy was a good driver, and with Lady Goodlad and Marie-Claire as extra lookouts, they made it into the heart of the city without incident.

In spite of the traffic, the beauty and splendor of Rome was awe-inspiring: wide avenues with vistas of ancient buildings, churches, and monuments; narrow, cobblestoned streets hosting elegant shops, galleries, and restaurants. Almost every corner boasted a fountain or a statue, and the flowers and trees were in riotous spring bloom. Arriving at their destination, Billy pulled the car up to the base of a magnificent flight of steps.

"The Piazza di Spagna—the Spanish Steps . . . ," Lady Goodlad explained. "Probably the most famous square in Rome. I'll get out here, Billy. The salon is just a few yards down the Via Condotti. Marie-Claire, perhaps you'd walk me there—and the shoe shop is just a couple of doors

away. I'll be fine once I'm in the hairdresser's. I'll be there for a couple of hours, and you two should go and have some fun." She cupped Bo's face in her hands, then tickled Panache under the chin. "Be good, little ones!"

While they waited for Marie-Claire to return, Billy, Bo, and Panache took in their extraordinary surroundings. At the top of the old stone steps was a majestic church with two domed bell towers, in front of which was a needle-shaped stone pillar. Banks of red azaleas decorated the multiple levels, which were bordered by graceful lampposts and tall, shuttered houses. At the bottom, a sunken fountain containing a statue of a leaking boat spouted water in all directions. Children sat on the rim, their bare feet dangling in the water. Shaded tables sold souvenirs and gelati to the tourists who thronged the area.

Marie-Claire had recommended that they see at least three places—St. Peter's Square, the Piazza Navona, and, above all, the Colosseum—so Billy mapped out a circular route on the navigation system that would encompass them all. When Marie-Claire returned, he said, "I know I'll want to stop at everything we see!"

She smiled. "With only two hours, we will do what we can."

They headed toward the famous Tiber River and drove across one of its antiquated bridges. Panache had fallen asleep, but Bo jumped onto the front seat and into Marie-Claire's lap and put her paws on the rim of the window in order to see better.

Arriving at a long avenue flanked with elegant lampposts and palms, Billy gasped at the vista before them.

"*C'est magnifique, n'est-ce pas?*" said Marie-Claire. "The Piazza San Pietro—and Saint Peter's Basilica. It is the largest and most beautiful church in the world. They say the great apostle is buried beneath it . . . and the pope lives just over there."

Bo saw a magnificent oval piazza, with another stone pillar at its center and cascading fountains either side. Around the perimeter were row upon row of white columns, topped by railings supporting a seemingly endless parade of stone figures. They gazed down over the piazza from every direction, including the façade of the great domed basilica. Bo thought that this person called Pope must be very special.

Marie-Claire said quietly, "I am *never* disappointed when I come here."

"I wish we could explore," Billy said after a moment.

"*Hélas*, it would take more than the two hours we have. Let us come back another time. Today we just make friends with the city."

Reluctantly, Billy turned the car around. "Piazza Navona, here we come."

"And I will buy you a gelato when we get there," promised Marie-Claire.

"Mmm! Reason enough to brave the traffic once again!" He turned off the main highway and drove down several narrow streets. "I'm not sure how much farther we can go. These alleys are so small—OOPS!" He braked to a sudden halt. Panache opened his eyes and Bo leaped onto the dashboard to see what was happening. Barring their way was a long line of steel barricades. "That does it!" said Billy. "There's no room to turn around . . . and, oh boy, here comes trouble."

An officious-looking policeman was walking toward the car. Dressed in a navy blue jacket, gray trousers with a red stripe down the side, and a wide, white belt and gloves, he imperiously raised a hand indicating they should stay where they were. Billy and Marie-Claire exchanged anxious looks, but then—to their surprise—the policeman pulled aside one of the barricades and, with a lot of theatrical arm waving, gestured they should drive the car on through.

Billy hesitated.

"Go, Billee, *go*!" Marie-Claire urged. "He is giving us permission!"

Billy inched the car forward, the policeman waving them on. Spotting Bo sitting on the dashboard, he bowed as though to a princess, then gave her a smart salute.

"Wow!" Billy grinned with impish delight. "What do you suppose *that* was about? Was it the diplomatic license plates, or did Bo charm him?"

"Perhaps a leetle of both!" Marie-Claire waved her thanks to the policeman as they drove away.

"Wait till I tell the skipper about this!" Billy laughed.

They emerged into the sunlight of the Piazza Navona, a long and lovely square with three magnificent fountains down the center. Canopied stalls

and tables with umbrellas and chairs were everywhere. Tourists perused the antique shops or took refreshments at sidewalk cafés; pigeons scuttled about, pecking at crumbs. Billy easily found a shady place to park—theirs was virtually the only car in the square, with the exception of an occasional delivery van.

"We can step out for one moment," Marie-Claire said, and placed Bo on the backseat next to Panache. Billy lowered the window a fraction, so the cats would get some air, and turned off the ignition. Exiting the car, he closed the door just as Bo attempted to follow him. He tapped a finger on the glass and said to her, "Back in a moment, Bo!" She peered through the window at him, her eyes wide as saucers, and meowed plaintively.

Panache stretched lazily. "Some adventure!" he said drowsily.

"Well, it *would* be if I was on my own!" Bo replied tartly.

The ginger cat blinked at her fondly. "You don't enjoy my company, *ma petite?*"

"Not at the moment," she replied haughtily. "Anyway, you've been asleep most of the time."

Panache reached out a paw, but she pushed him away and turned back to the window, watching as Marie-Claire and Billy stopped at a nearby stall to purchase their gelati. She saw them cross to the impressive center fountain, resplendent with a huge piece of granite, statues of godlike figures and animals, and yet another tall, slender column in the center. Water

spewed and splashed in all directions.

"These needle things seem to be everywhere in Rome!" Billy observed.

"*Oui*, they are called obelisks," Marie-Claire explained. "Egyptian, originally, but popular also in ancient Rome. They say if you throw money into the fountain and make a wish, it will come true." Extracting a coin from her purse, she closed her eyes for a moment, then tossed it into the sparkling water.

Gazing at her sweet face, Billy knew exactly what his wish would be. Producing his own coin, he threw it in next to hers.

Bo cheered up the minute Billy and Marie-Claire returned.

Marie-Claire checked her watch. "We still have time before we pick up Her Ladyship. Let us drive to the Colosseum, Billee—you must see it."

"*Votre désir est mon plaisir!*" Billy said, trying out his French with an excruciating English accent.

"What?"

"Your wish is my command."

Marie-Claire collapsed with the giggles. Panache looked at Bo and yawned.

CHAPTER NINE

The Colosseum

THE MASSIVE RUIN OF the Colosseum was as impressive as Marie-Claire had described. Four stories high, the crumbling façade was ringed with open arches, backlit by the afternoon sun.

"My word," Billy marveled. "It is splendid! Imagine what it must have been like in the old days. . . . " He reached for his guidebook. "'A public arena where gladiators once fought for the entertainment of the people; where wild beasts of every sort from all over the world were added to the spectacle.'" He snapped the book shut. "Oh, Marie-Claire, we *have* to go inside and see the rest!"

She nodded. "We will take a quick peek—but let us hurry!"

Bo realized that once again she and Panache were going to be left in the car. She jumped onto the rear-window ledge and gazed despairingly after Marie-Claire and Billy as they disappeared into the throng of tourists entering the ruin.

"*Bof!*" Panache exclaimed. "*This* one I would have liked to see."

"I don't understand," said Bo. "Billy used to take me everywhere. Look! There's a cat, going through that archway! Obviously cats are

allowed in. . . ."

Panache placed his paws on the armrest of the door and pressed his nose to the crack of the slightly open window. He sniffed and nudged at it. "Not enough room for a mouse to squeeze through," he muttered.

Suddenly there was a soft hum, and the window slid all the way down.

Bo and Panache looked at each other.

"What did you *do?*" asked Bo in surprise.

"I don't know!" Panache was puzzled. "But let's go, *eh?* Before the window changes its mind! We will never have another chance!"

"And we'll find Billy inside!" Bo concurred.

They sprang out of the car and scampered across the cobblestones.

There were so many people gathered about the entrance that it was impossible for the cats to see much of anything. Panache darted through the crowd and into the arena. Bo followed as he leaped onto a big wedge of granite, and the interior of the Colosseum was suddenly revealed to them both.

It was a vast oval space, open to the skies, with tier after tier of crumbling stone arches, curved passages, and low walls, worn smooth over the centuries yet with an awesome majesty and strength.

In the center of the arena, a large pit two stories deep encompassed the ruins of underground tunnels and walls. Spanning it was a narrow modern walkway.

Bo was reminded of the ring at the circus, though that now seemed tiny in comparison with this.

"Extraordinaire!" Panache murmured. Bo wondered if Papa had ever been to this amazing place.

Some tourists spotted the two cats and came toward them.

"Uh-oh! Quickly, *ma petite!*" Panache warned. "This way!"

Evading the grasping hands, they jumped down and scampered along the perimeter of the ring.

"I don't see Billy," Bo panted. "We *should* try to find him. . . . He was only going to be here a few minutes." She scanned the tiered galleries, where more people were exploring. "Do you suppose he's up there?"

"Or perhaps down below, in the center," Panache suggested. "Let's try that first."

Carefully, with Bo following, he made his way to a lower ledge, and then another, until they reached a grass patch on the lowest level of the Colosseum.

They walked around, exploring the mazelike avenues of ancient tunnels and rooms, but there was no sign of Billy and Marie-Claire.

"Maybe we shouldn't have done this," Bo said, beginning to feel uneasy. "What if they have gone back to the car by now?"

"C'est possible," Panache agreed. "We'll go look." He stood uncertainly, sniffing the air. "But where did we come in?"

They tried to find their way to the main entrance, but the more they wandered, the more confused and disoriented they became.

Hot and thirsty, Bo was now truly anxious.

"Courage, chérie!" said Panache. "We will soon be out of here."

Rounding a corner, they suddenly spotted a white cat with black-tipped ears sunning herself on a slab of stone.

"Let's ask her for help!" Bo said, relieved.

Adopting a casual manner, Panache sauntered toward the snoozing feline. "*Scusi, signora,*" he said in his best attempt at Italian. The cat opened her eyes, which were a beautiful shade of primrose yellow. "*Perdoname* for—er—interrupting your *siesta,* but could you—um—*diretto* us to the gate?"

"There are many gates," she replied in a kindly voice.

"Oh! You speak English," Panache said, relieved.

"Thousands who come here speak English," she replied. "One learns a little."

"We're looking for the big gate," said Bo, joining them. "The one where the cars are parked."

The white cat stood up and stretched. "I will show you. You will never find it by yourself."

Something about this cat compelled respect, and dipping his head, Panache said, "*Grazie.* You are very gracious."

* * *

They followed their new guide, and Panache and Bo learned that her name was Hepzibah, and that she was one of many cats who called the Colosseum home.

"But who looks after you? Who feeds you?" Bo was puzzled.

"We look after ourselves," Hepzibah answered. "And the *gattini* are very good to us."

Before Bo had time to ask what that word meant, Panache said, "There! That is the gate we came in!"

Bo raced ahead of him into the parking lot, only to come to an abrupt halt. Billy and Marie-Claire were nowhere in sight. Worse still, the car had disappeared. In fact, the parking lot was almost empty.

"They're gone!" Bo cried. "Panache! They're not here!"

She ran back and forth frantically, hoping that perhaps she would find them in a different spot.

"*Maugrebleu!*" Panache sat down. "Now what?"

"If you hadn't been in such a hurry to have an adventure . . . ," Bo said, somewhat unfairly. The ginger cat looked crestfallen, but seeing

her distress he wisely said nothing.

"I can help?" asked Hepzibah.

"I don't think so," Bo replied, but poured out her story anyway, adding, "So you see, I may never see my Billy again. Oh—and he must be *so* worried about me!" she wailed.

Hepzibah said gently, "There may still be some hope. A little child became lost here the other day, but eventually his parents found him. So, if you wait . . . And tonight we have an assembly of all the cats. Our consul, Magnus, will have some ideas. But here is our *gattina*. Are you hungry?"

An old woman pushing a shopping cart was walking toward them. Crooning soft words in Italian, she produced some paper plates and filled them with scraps of food. Panache and Bo shared a dish, and Hepzibah ate from the other, carefully setting aside a small piece of chicken on the cobblestones. The kind lady filled a bowl with water, and when the cats had drunk their fill, she packed up everything and moved on.

"She will feed a lot of us by the end of the day," Hepzibah explained,

watching her go. "Many good cat people—the *gattini*—come to feed us, and we are grateful."

"Well, it certainly gets the spot," Panache confessed, licking his whiskers.

Hepzibah said, "Now we should return. One of our family is not well, and I must take her this food. You would be wise to come with me." She picked up the morsel of chicken and walked back into the arena.

Panache said, "She's right, Bo. We will be safer with her. And Billy will come back." Reluctantly, with a glance over her shoulder, Bo followed the others and slipped through the gate just as a guard was locking it for the evening.

Hepzibah led them across the central walkway of the now-deserted amphitheater. Reaching the platform on the other side, she said, "Wait here."

The shadows lengthened. Clouds began to form overhead, and the sun became a burnished copper red. The empty Colosseum now seemed bigger than ever and had a mournful, ghostly aspect to it. Bo fancied she heard the snarl of a lion, the clash of swords and ringing of steel, the roar of a bloodthirsty crowd. As darkness descended, she pressed close to Panache, glad of his company. He, too, seemed ill at ease, and the fur on his back began to bristle, as a soft whispering came from all sides, as if ancient Roman spirits were gathering. The whispering became a low growl, which grew louder and louder. Then they saw the eyes—hundreds of them, on all sides, glowing in the darkness.

Bo and Panache spun in circles to face whatever demons were about to confront them. As they did so, the Colosseum's night illuminations suddenly blazed into life, bathing the arena with a golden light and revealing that they were surrounded by cats—scores of them, of every shape, size, and color.

CHAPTER TEN

The Fight

A LARGE, MUSCULAR cat stepped from the ranks and stood contemplating Bo and Panache with a disdainful eye. He was superbly fit, silver black with prominent ears and a fine nose. Muscles rippled beneath his shiny fur. He was flanked by two other cats, clearly subservient to him.

"*Sono* Titus," he said. "*E voi?*"

"*Sono* Panache." The ginger cat met his gaze.

"What is your business here?"

"No business, *mio amico*. We came as visitors and have lost our way."

"How careless . . . especially in the company of one so attractive." Titus made a slow circle around Bo and called to one of his cohorts. "*Che bella, eh,* Flavius?" He brushed Bo lightly with his tail. "*Angelo mio,* such eyes!"

The cat called Flavius joined Titus. "*Madonna . . . ,*" he crooned to Bo. "*Guarda, Canio!* Look!" The other cohort sauntered over, and pushing Panache out of his way, he sidled up to Bo. "*Ciao, bambina!*" he said provocatively. When Bo pulled back, the three cats pressed closer and she was trapped between them.

Flavius growled his approval.

Canio said, *"Che amore!"*

Titus laughed, and spurred on by catcalls and taunting remarks from the crowd, the three bullies continued to tease and provoke. The more Bo shrank from their attentions, the more delighted they seemed.

There was a blur of ginger color as Panache leaped in front of Bo, his fur fluffed and his tail whipping from side to side.

"Step away from the lady," he said quietly, but there was no mistaking his rage.

Titus looked surprised. His two companions arched their backs and hissed at Panache with annoyance. The crowd gasped and fell silent.

"Aha! The goddess has a watchdog!" Titus sneered. "She becomes more interesting by the minute!"

Panache stood his ground. "I'm serious. Leave the lady alone."

Flavius and Canio crouched low, looking to Titus for the command to spring, but

Titus—without taking his eyes off Panache—said, "I'll handle this." He paused for a moment, taut with anticipation, then said, "*D'accordo*, watchdog . . . *make* me."

There was a murmur of excitement from the crowd. "A game! A game!" The many cats pressed together tightly to form an impenetrable circle.

"Be careful, Panache!" Bo whimpered. For a split second, nothing happened—and then Titus leaped for Panache with claws unfurled.

The Colosseum was suddenly alive with sound as the two cats collided, shrieking and yowling with rage, and the crowd roared its approval. The fighters were so quick, it was hard to distinguish one from the other, and the fur flew as each grappled for supremacy. With neither gaining the upper hand, they broke apart.

Titus swiped a paw at Panache's face, but the ginger cat deftly avoided it and countered with a blow of his own, which grazed Titus's shoulder.

"*Beh!*" Titus shrugged. "Is that the best you can do?"

The powerful silver black cat lunged forward, but Panache rolled neatly to one side. Titus spun around to face his adversary, and the feral crowd urged him on. "*Vai!* Go! Go!"

Titus and Panache engaged again, rolling over and over, biting, scratching, and snarling at each other. Bo, her heart pounding, cried out as Titus pinned Panache to the ground and went for his throat—but Panache twisted away, and the black cat bit his ear instead, drawing blood. Clearly, Titus was the bigger and more powerful of the two, but what Panache lacked in stature he made up for in dexterity and timing. Using his back legs, he raked his claws across Titus's belly, and as the big cat drew up in pain, he threw him off.

Leaping onto Titus's back, Panache bit into the scruff of his neck and held on tight. The two spun around and around, until Titus reared up and finally rid himself of his challenger with a mighty shrug. He slammed Panache to the ground, knocking the wind out of him. Panache scrambled to his feet, and for a moment the cats were nose to nose, eyes blazing and teeth bared. Titus's claws, like deadly weapons, aimed for Panache's eyes, and, breathless, Panache was forced backward, ducking this way and that, avoiding the razor-sharp blades by only a fraction.

Gradually, the bigger cat pressed home the advantage of his considerable strength and weight and, exhausted, Panache's legs suddenly buckled beneath him.

The inflamed crowd cheered Titus on with bloodthirsty cries of "*Ora! Ora!* NOW!"

"Do you admit defeat?" Titus hissed, standing over Panache, one paw on his chest.

"And leave Bo with you? *Never!*"

For a split second, Titus glanced at Bo—and Panache seized his opportunity. Wrapping his tired legs around Titus's neck and gripping tightly, he sank his teeth into the soft tissue of the black cat's throat. Titus yowled in pain, and Panache shouldered him to one side, then rolled on top of the larger cat to gain supremacy at the last moment.

There was a shocked silence, followed by a roar of acclaim from the onlookers. Bo rushed to Panache's side, and Titus struggled to his feet, beaten and bruised. Suddenly, surprisingly, the crowd broke ranks to allow an elegant, distinguished-looking cat to enter the circle.

The newcomer was obviously a senior member of the pack, for the attitude toward him on all sides was one of great respect. He had warm

chestnut brown fur and steady green eyes. His furrowed brow and intelligent face gave the impression of a wise elder who had seen and heard much. He stood alone, assessing the scene in front of him.

Finally, he spoke.

"Have we become barbarians once again? Who started this?"

Canio stepped forward. "Great Magnus, we have strangers in our midst. . . ."

"Titus was managing the situation, my lord. It got out of control," Flavius joined in.

"I think he can speak for himself," said Magnus. "What say you, Titus?"

The silver black cat took a deep breath, steadied himself, then bowed. "No harm done, Magnus. A minor scrap, that's all. A misunderstanding."

Hepzibah pushed through the crowd.

"My lord," she said. "These *stranieri*—visitors—were abandoned here

today. I suggested they wait with us to see if their family returns for them."

"And this is the welcome they received? We may be an independent society, but we are not uncivilized." Magnus turned to Panache and Bo. "My apologies, friends. It seems my hotheaded tribune has represented us badly."

"No apology necessary," Panache replied graciously. "As Titus said, no harm done."

The crowd murmured its approval.

Magnus turned to Titus with a questioning glance. After a moment, Titus spoke, a new respect in his voice.

"You are welcome, friend," he said to Panache. "I salute you."

Hepzibah stepped forward.

"My lord," she said with a tone of urgency, "I came to tell you that the ailing one's condition has worsened. I am at a loss. . . . "

Magnus nodded. "We will go to her immediately. Come, friends," he said to Panache and Bo. "You will stay as our guests. It is the least we can do."

CHAPTER ELEVEN

The Invalid

THEY FOLLOWED MAGNUS, Hepzibah, Titus, and the other cats into the lower depths of the arena.

Bo whispered to Panache, "Are you all right? Are you hurt? I was so worried!"

"*Pouf!*" Panache shrugged. "A couple of scratches. I was lucky." He chuckled. "So, we have an adventure after all!"

Bo pressed against him with affection. "Not the kind I like," she said. "I'm sorry I was ratty with you earlier. You were so brave tonight."

Magnus led them all to a small chamber deep within the cavernous ruin. In the far corner, a small bundle was lying on a weather-beaten scrap of toweling. It was a black-and-white cat, so thin her ribs were visible through her mangy fur.

Hepzibah spoke to her gently. "My dear, here is Magnus. Can you speak to him? You have not touched the food I brought you."

"I cannot . . . ," the frail cat whispered.

Bo felt the skin on the back of her neck prickle. She ventured closer, suddenly eager to see the invalid more clearly. Recognizing the three white paws and the white blaze on her nose, Bo felt her heart skip a beat.

"Polly?" she said incredulously. "Oh, *Polly*! It's Bo!"

The black and white cat struggled to lift her head. "Boadicea? My little Bo? Is it really you?"

Bo turned to the others with excitement. "I know this cat! She is my sister Polly!" She crouched beside Polly, and the two cats nuzzled each other affectionately. "I was so hoping I would find you! I've been looking for you. But what ails you, my dear? And how do you come to be *here*? I saw Samson at the circus, and he told me that you were in Italy, but that you had met someone and run away. . . ."

Polly sighed wearily. "I was foolish. I thought I had found my true love, but he abandoned me in Sienna. I became heartsick, and lost my appetite for food and for life. I wandered for days until a kindly student picked me up and left me at the Colosseum. I think he knew that someone here would take care of me. . . ." She gazed at Hepzibah and Magnus with gratitude. "And they have. They've tried their best."

Bo nudged the piece of chicken closer to her sister. "Eat, dear Polly. It will help you."

"But what about you, Bo?" Polly asked weakly. "What brings *you* to Italy?"

As her sister nibbled at tiny morsels of chicken, Bo told her story. She explained about Billy, the adventures that had brought them from England through France—where she had met up with Tubs—and finally here to

Rome. She spoke of the Goodlads and the beautiful *Legend*. She introduced Panache and described how they had just become separated from Billy. "If only he were here, Polly," she added, "he would know how to help you; I know he would."

"What was the purpose of his visit to Rome?" asked Magnus thoughtfully.

Panache suddenly became alert. "There was an *affaire* the Goodlads had to attend. . . ."

"When?"

"Tonight!" Bo added excitedly. "At someplace—British! It had British in the name!"

Magnus dipped his head in thought, then looked up. "The British embassy?" he suggested.

"*Ambassador!*" Panache cried excitedly. "The British ambassador's villa! *C'est ça!*"

"But he lives very close to here," Magnus declared. "I pass the villa often. We could show you the way."

"Oh, Polly!" Bo cried. "Do you think you could make it there? Can you walk?"

Polly whispered, "I am too weak."

Titus stepped out of the shadows. "I can help. I will carry her."

Magnus nodded approvingly. "A noble gesture. It shall be so."

"We must leave at once," said Hepzibah. "We have no time to lose."

Gently lifting Polly by the scruff of her neck, the powerful Titus carried her as if she were a mere kitten. The other cats fell into step behind him, and as they made their way through the Colosseum, they were joined by more cats, and more still, until a phalanx of them emerged onto the roadway under the night sky.

They paused occasionally to allow Titus and Polly the chance to rest. At one point, Panache stepped forward and said to Titus, "Allow me." As the ginger cat took a turn carrying Polly, Bo trotted beside him, murmuring encouraging words to her sister. One by one, members of the feral pack introduced themselves.

"I am Augustus," said one. "We will soon be there!"

"Obadiah," said a scruffy calico. "Not long now!"

"Balthazar!" said another. Then, to Panache, "You fought bravely to-night!"

Others came forward—Dominicus, Hadrian, Septimus, Boaz. Three almost identical tabbies spoke as one: "Shadrach, Meshach, and Abednego!"

What had recently been a raging, unruly crowd was now a unified team, showing only respect for their guests and focusing on a common purpose.

Finally, Magnus came to a halt beside a high wall. From behind it, faint music and the chatter of voices could be heard. "This is as far as we can take you. The gate is there. You can see the guard. Our good wishes go with you."

Titus gently placed Polly on the ground.

Bo said, "Great Magnus, our thanks to you—to Hepzibah—to *all*. We shall never forget your kindness."

Titus confided to Panache, "I was wrong to behave as I did earlier. I am grateful for your tact on the matter."

Panache shrugged amiably. "*De rien.* I believe if we should meet again, it will be as friends."

Hepzibah touched Bo lovingly, then bent to speak to Polly, who lay still as a stone, her eyes vacant with exhaustion. "Take heart, little one—all will be well, I am sure of it."

The sound of footsteps on the sidewalk indicated someone was approaching. The cats of the Colosseum wheeled as one, and with a mere whisper of sound they melted into the shadows, leaving Bo, Panache, and Polly alone in the dark night.

The footsteps drew nearer, and two people came into view, conversing animatedly.

"This is the place, Fred," said one. "Sounds like some party! Now, how do we get in?" Catching sight of the three cats, he said, "Hang about! Isn't that the kitty-cat I like? The one from the Goodlads' boat?"

"My word! It is!" said the other. "What a bit of luck!"

"Well! Now we know the Goodlads are here," said the first. With a pang of dismay, Bo realized that the two men were none other than Jack Haggard and Fred Pallid. Before she could say anything to Panache, Jack's coarse hands scooped her up. "Kootchy-coo!" he said, scratching her roughly under the chin. "What are you doing out here, Puss? You're missing all the fun!"

"Here, I've got an idea!" said Fred excitedly. "Follow me!"

He strolled nonchalantly up to the policeman who was guarding the gate.

"Excusa-me, signoro. We've got a bit of a situation. This cat belongs to one of your guests inside, and they may have been searching for her."

"That's right." Jack joined him. "The name's Goodlad. Have a look on your list and see if we're not right."

The policeman looked confused, and Jack pressed his point.

"You don't have to take our word for it, mate. Get on the wire and ask if they're missing a cat. You'll be glad you did."

Somewhat reluctantly, the policeman removed a walkie-talkie from his belt and spoke into it in rapid Italian. After repeating himself several times, he nodded. Holding up a hand to Haggard and Pallid, he said, "*Aspettate.* You wait. Someone comes."

"There you are," Fred declared. "What did we tell you?"

Bo's heart soared with relief as she heard Lady Goodlad's voice coming down the drive.

"I don't care, Barney! I'm coming with you! Just give them whatever they ask, as long as we get the cats back!"

"I'll handle this, Jessie," Lord Goodlad replied as they arrived at the gate, escorted by a member of the ambassador's staff. "Now, what's going on?"

Lady Goodlad cried out as she recognized Bo. "There! It *is* her!" Running forward, she scooped Bo out of Haggard's arms. "Oh, what a relief! Billy will be *so* thrilled!"

Recognizing Haggard and Pallid, Lord Goodlad said, "Wait a moment! We've met before! Aren't you the gentlemen who were at the restaurant in the South of France when Jessie was nearly kidnapped? What an amazing coincidence!"

"Isn't it just!" said Haggard. "We happened to be passing, and suddenly there was your cat, on the sidewalk!"

Lady Goodlad looked down, for Panache was weaving around her legs, meowing and purring. "Look! They're *both* here! Where have you been, you rascal? We thought someone had taken you!" As she bent to stroke him, he ran a few yards back toward Polly, who was still lying on the ground.

"What is it, fellow? What have you found?" she asked, noticing the listless shape on the ground. "Good heavens, it's another cat! Barney, come and look—I don't think she's well at all!"

"Now, Jessie . . ."

"No, no!" Lady Goodlad interrupted. "She's barely alive. Barney, we must *do* something!"

"Do something about what?" A distinguished-looking gentleman joined them.

"Oh, Ambassador! The most extraordinary thing has happened! You

96

heard about our two missing cats—well, here they are! These kind people found them for us! And there's another little cat—she's terribly unwell! Is there someone you could call?"

"Jessie, the streets of Rome are filled with cats!" Lord Goodlad said with some impatience. "Do you to intend to rescue them *all*?"

"Not to worry, Barney," the ambassador said reassuringly. "We'll phone the vet. He's a decent fellow, and I think he'll want to check this one anyway." Turning to his aide, he said, "Bring them all in, and ask Dr. Baldini to make a house call."

"We should let Billy know as well," Lady Goodlad added. "He and Marie-Claire have been at the police station all evening, sick with worry." She looked at Haggard and Pallid. "You've done us the most enormous courtesy. How can we possibly thank you?"

"Come in, come in!" said the ambassador. "A glass of champagne at least." He turned to the policeman. "*Molte grazie,* Fulvio. You did well."

They all headed for the villa. Bringing up the rear, Haggard and Pallid winked at each other, caught the eye of the policeman, and gave him a thumbs-up.

CHAPTER TWELVE

A Celebration

BILLY WAS ECSTATIC when he heard the good news about Bo and Panache. He and Marie-Claire rushed back from the police station, and he swept Bo into his arms.

"Oh, my Bonnie! My little Bo—how did you get lost? How did you find your way here? If only you could speak! No matter—you're safe now."

Bo purred affectionately and kneaded his jacket with her paws.

Billy stroked Panache. "Hello, my fine fellow! What happened to your ear? What on earth have you two been doing?"

Everyone gathered in the library. The cats were given food and milk, and the vet arrived. The ambassador's wife presided over the activities with Lady Goodlad, and was particularly taken with the little black and white cat who seemed so ill.

"Poor little thing! What could have happened to her? She reminds me of my Fluffy, when I was five years old!"

Billy turned to Haggard and Pallid. "I cannot thank you enough!" he said. "I've been beside myself with worry! We were in the Colosseum for just a moment, came back to the car, and found the window wide open and the cats gone. We searched and searched without success. Lady Goodlad was sure they had been stolen. I think everyone at the police station thought we were quite mad. . . ." Billy laughed, giddy with delight. "They said that looking for a lost cat in Rome was like looking for a needle in a haystack. But you two found them for us! How extraordinary that you happened to be here, tonight, when the last we saw each other was on the quay in the South of France!"

Dr. Baldini removed the stethoscope from his ears and laid a gentle hand on Polly. "She will be fine," he said. "But she needs *antibiotici*. I take her with me to the *clinica* for a few days."

"Please let me know when she's better," said the ambassador's wife. "I'd really like to give her a home here."

"*Bene*." The vet nodded. Turning his attention to Panache, he said, "Now we look at the ear of this *bello gatto*. . . ."

He expertly swabbed Panache's caked and bloodied wound, and the ginger cat winced a little, then grinned at Bo. "*Alors*, we've had an *excellent* adventure!"

Bo gazed at him lovingly. "And *you* are an excellent friend," she said.

Touching Polly's nose with her own, she whispered, "You're going to be fine, Polly. You'll have a good home here at the ambassador's house, and I'm sure we'll meet again! Did I mention that Samson's circus is coming to Rome? If you can—when you can—try to let him know that you are safe."

"They are *so* adorable!" Lady Goodlad murmured as the two cats nuzzled each other.

The ambassador tapped his champagne glass with a spoon to get everyone's attention. "I think a toast is in order!" he said jovially, and he raised his glass to Haggard and Pallid. "To the little cats and their rescuers! And to my dear friends Barney and Jessie . . . the happiest couple I know. We hope you'll visit again soon. Here's to fair winds and a much-deserved respite in the Greek islands."

"Hear, hear!" everyone echoed, and there was the sound of ringing crystal as glasses touched together. Haggard elbowed Pallid in the ribs, and they exchanged meaningful looks.

"Now—a surprise!" said the ambassador. "Let us join the other guests outside. The great soprano Bella Cantolini has agreed to favor us with a song."

He led the way to an attractive stone terrace. It was decorated with potted lemon trees, fragrant in the night air. Delicate gilt chairs were arranged to face a small chamber orchestra. Two curving staircases led to the gardens and a fountain beyond.

As Billy and Marie-Claire took their seats, with Bo in his arms and

Panache in hers, Billy said to Jack Haggard and Fred Pallid, "I'm still puzzled as to how you just happened to be here tonight."

Haggard hesitated. "Ah, well," he said. "Yes! We were—er—we *are* en route to Naples, Capri, Venice—a business trip."

Pallid nodded. "Lots of water around Italy, you know!"

"And—Fred's passport had expired," Haggard went on. "We were hoping the ambassador here could help facilitate a renewal."

Billy looked puzzled. "But how did you know—" he began, but his words were drowned by applause as Bella Cantolini swept onto the terrace.

The famous diva was swathed in yards of yellow chiffon, a silk handkerchief clutched in one hand. She bowed as the orchestra played her

introduction, then took a deep breath and began to sing in a plummy voice. By the third aria, Lord Goodlad, stifling a yawn, began to nod off, and even Billy felt his eyelids heavy after such a long and adventurous day.

As Signora Cantolini's voice echoed across the gardens, Bo and Panache became aware of another sound—a faint caterwauling from the surrounding trees and rooftops. It was their friends from the Colosseum, yowling and meowing in harmony with the music.

In the car on the way back to *Legend*, Lord Goodlad chuckled. "We must tell the captain the events of this day for the ship's log. It's certainly been one to remember!"

"You know, it's odd about those two . . . Haggard and Pallid," Billy said. "At first I didn't trust them. Now I suppose I'll be forever grateful to them." He glanced in the rearview mirror and saw Bo and Panache snuggled blissfully on the backseat between Lady Goodlad and Marie-Claire. Billy lowered his voice. "But I meant to mention to you, sir, that they came by the yacht just before we left the South of France. They seemed oddly shifty—asked a lot of questions as to where we were going. The funny thing is I didn't tell them we were coming to Rome. . . . so how did they know that you would be at the ambassador's villa tonight?"

"Hmm." Lord Goodlad looked thoughtful. "It does seem rather strange . . . the coincidence of it all. Truthfully, I didn't take to them much myself. I've learned, Billy, that one's first instincts can generally be trusted. Anyway, we'll be weighing anchor again tomorrow, so we'll soon be miles away and that's probably the last we'll ever see of them."

"Aye aye, sir."

Bo was happy to hear the news. She felt warm and cozy, and so relieved to be with her beloved Billy again. How wonderful it was to know that Polly was safe and had found a good home, just like Samson and Tubs! If only she could tell Mama and Papa. Now, if she could just find Maximillian . . .

But that was an adventure for another day.

Little Bo, a tiny gray cat with a big name—
Bonnie Boadicea—lives a life of big adventure.
Join in her journey with

Little Bo and
Little Bo in France

Other books by Julie Andrews Edwards
& Emma Walton Hamilton

Thanks to You: Wisdom from Mother & Child
The Great American Mousical
Simeon's Gift
Dragon: Hound of Honor

and the Dumpy the Dumptruck books:

Dumpy and the Firefighters
Dumpy to the Rescue!
Dumpy's Apple Shop
Dumpy's Extra-Busy Day
Dumpy's Happy Holiday
Dumpy's Valentine